Ron,

It was great talking with you. Now write the book you have inside you!

John Rull
12/8/07

The Diary
of
Josiah Webb

John Ruhl

M**AJOR**M**ICRO**P**RESS**

The Diary of Josiah Webb

by

John Ruhl

First Edition Copyright 2005

Published by:

MajorMicro Press
3579 Huntley Terrace
Crete, IL 60417-1303
www.majormicropress.com
708-672-3089

ISBN 0-9765921-0-X

Library of Congress Control Number:
2005922744

Preface

I'm a writer by trade, but a baseball card collector in my heart, an addiction I acquired late in life. When my grandmother told me a few months ago that she thought my father might have some cards still stashed in her attic, it took me about five minutes to drive over to her house and start sifting through boxes of mostly junk, with visions of Honus Wagner in my mind. Most kids' mothers would have thrown out this stuff as soon as the kids left the nest, but my grandmother is a saver. Perhaps my father not coming home from Korea was responsible for her hanging on to his junk this long, but whatever the reason, I was sure I would find a buried treasure in his old baseball card collection.

I did find a few cards in a cigar box, mostly of players I had never heard of, and most of which were torn and creased from their primary purpose of turning a bicycle into a motorcycle by clothes-pinning them against the wheel spokes. Never the less, I was happy to find this glimpse of the past, regardless of its value or lack thereof. Card collecting was fun to me more because of that mystical connection to the past than for any investment potential that might be there.

This same fascination with the past piqued my curiosity when I ran across the crumbling cardboard box tied together with a brittle ribbon. I recognized my great grandfather's name, Hiram Ruhl, written on the lid in a shaky cursive script. I quickly forgot about the baseball cards as I began to read the contents of the box.

Darkness fell as the story in the box unfolded. My grandmother had given up on me and long since eaten her supper by the time I descended the stairs with the treasures under my arm. She had been unaware of her father-in-law's box or the story it contained and was as fascinated as I had been as I told her what I had found and briefly related what I had read. Her eyesight was poor, and it was late, so I promised to come back the next evening to read to her my great grandfather's story.

I did as agreed, and the following evening we opened the box again and pored over pieces of our history never known to anyone but my great grandfather. The box contained a yellowing typed manuscript, a journal, and quite a few letters. I knew from the previous night that the journal and all the letters had been reproduced in the manuscript, so after showing everything to my grandmother, I began to read to her from page one of the manuscript. About half way through, I suggested that she was probably tired and that I would be glad to finish reading to her the next night. She wouldn't let me stop. I was painting for her a picture of a side of her father-in-law that she had never known, and she wanted to know it all. Misty eyes had turned to flowing tears for both of us by the time I finished.

Hiram Ruhl never intended for anyone else to read his manuscript. He lived some thirty years after he wrote it, and the box remained undiscovered for another forty years as it gathered dust in the attic. I asked my grandmother what she thought about me getting the manuscript published, and I no sooner had suggested it than it became her passion. Had I not agreed to see this story through to printing, I have no doubt that somehow she would have done it herself.

What follows is Hiram's manuscript. I have embellished only minor details to make it more readable. Writers have a hard time denying themselves this license. Those embellishments should be very obvious once the complete story is read. The story itself is Hiram's; I have changed nothing of the story line or of the sincerity that was poured into the manuscript and the journal and letters on which it was based.

John Ruhl
February 20, 2004

Hiram's Manuscript

Foreword

Josiah Webb was my best friend. My earliest memories include him....the two of us running barefoot on the wooden sidewalk to his father's general store, the penny licorice we always got from his father behind the counter, the dreaded day at age six when we had to put on our new shoes and trudge off to our first day of school, then, finally, summer vacation. Oh, how we lived for summers after that. The endless days spent in grade school are a blur now, but sometimes I think I can remember every minute and every adventure of every summer. And Josiah is indelibly etched into each of those memories as he now is in my soul.

We were two of the few in our class who were fortunate enough not only to finish high school, but to go on to college, together of course. We had both been fascinated by the sciences, and he eventually became a pharmacist, occupying a shop adjacent to his father's store. Coaxed, or perhaps more accurately described, coerced by my own father, I became a banker, and started my career across Main Street from the Webbs'. I'm still there today, in the corner office now. I thank my father now for the coercion. It kept me at home, to fulfill my destiny, to complete the one task for which I had been born, to help my best friend die.

When he got the news, at the ripe old age of thirty-four, that he wouldn't see thirty-five, I was the next to know. His wife found out a few shots of Jack Daniels later. Pharmacists had ready access to such improprieties, for medicinal purposes, even during Prohibition. His five-year-old son would barely know him, but as his godfather I tried to let him know his father as the father I knew he would have been.

Shortly after Josiah died, Molly brought me a sealed box with my name written on the lid in the shaky scrawl of Josiah's final days. When she left, I opened the box to find a note to me, a bound personal journal and several opened envelopes containing letters. In the pages that follow, I have reproduced Josiah's note to me, and his journal, with the letters inserted chronologically. Perhaps you will be able to read them dry-eyed, an accomplishment I have yet to achieve despite the years that have passed.

Hiram Ruhl
July 26, 1934

Note from Josiah –

June 28, 1924

Dear Hiram,

    It's no secret to either of us that I have very few days left, and I must share this story with you while I am able. You have been my friend for life, even in these past few months as I have withered away to another person. I have appreciated that, even if I was never able to adequately express it.

    I must first apologize if I have seemed distracted lately. I have indeed had other things on my mind. I have been caught up in an adventure of sorts, one that I have not shared with anyone, not even you, my trusted friend, for reasons that I hope will be understood. Soon after my adventure began, I decided it should be recorded, so I started a diary. I am now entrusting it to you, to do with as you see fit. I fear that my judgment is not to be trusted anymore, so it's up to you now to decide if the story survives.

    We will already have said our good-byes by the time you receive this, so I won't linger on morbid farewells. I regret leaving you as much as I regret anything, including not seeing my son become a man, and leaving my dear Molly to fend for herself. I know she will survive, because, in her own way, she is a stronger person than I am or was. She has shown me that, especially in these last months. You will all be with me, as I will be with you, in your hearts for now, until we are all together again.

Enough of that. I have been very diligent in keeping my diary, so I don't think I need to preface it. The story will tell itself if you read the accompanying letters as they are noted in the journal.

Godspeed, my friend.

Josiah

The Diary

Chapter 1

Diary Entry

May 20, 1924

My name is Josiah Byron Webb, and I was born January 13, 1890 in the house in which I live and undoubtedly will die. The latter I state with the confidence provided by the doctors who diagnosed the cancer which has taken over my body, but which has thus far avoided my mind. I have accepted my fate, unwillingly at first, but now with little remorse. This I owe, in large part, to my great grandson, who has become my penpal. You have probably done the arithmetic with the dates above and know that I am thirty- four years old, too young to have a great grandson. An even less believable fact is that the great grandson with whom I write is himself forty-three, and his father has not yet been born.

I received his first letter on April 3, 1924, about six weeks ago, delivered by the postman with the rest of my mail. I noticed that the envelope had no return address, but otherwise was undistinguishable from the other mail. I am keeping the letters in the same box with this diary. You may want to read it now before you proceed with my next entry. I have penciled the date of receipt on each envelope and letter.

Letter 1, received April 3, 1924

June 26, 2003

Mr. Josiah Webb
301 N. Main Street
Nappanee, Indiana

Dear Josiah,

I hope that you can read this letter and accept it at face value, but as I write this, I'm not sure how I could persuade you that this is not a practical joke. I will try the truth and hope that the sincerity is apparent.

My name is Nathan Josiah Webb, and I am your great grandson. As you can see by the date on this letter, I am writing this in the year 2003. I live in the same house you live in in

1924, the same house where your son grew up. I am an electrophysicist, a profession which hardly exists yet as you read this. My specialty is research into the science of time. I have always been interested in time travel, a nagging quirk in my personality which I suspect is in my genes. I base this suspicion on the several volumes of science fiction books on my shelf, all of which have your name written inside the cover. Included among them, nearly falling apart now from having been reread so many times by, I suspect, you and your son and grandson, is H.G. Wells' The Time Machine.

Forgive me if the technical details are boring, and I promise I will be as brief as I can, but I really think some details are necessary if you are to understand how and why I am writing to you.

My Life's Work, A.L.T.

By the time I left college, I had a Ph.D. in electrophysics and went to work for General Electric. The government will finance anything that has any military potential, so I have found myself since then with virtually unlimited financing by way of federal grants in the guise of medical research.

For the last two years I have had a great deal of success in one project which I consider to be key to achieving time travel. The phenomenon I have concentrated on is called Atomic Level Transporting (A.L.T.), and in a nutshell involves disassembling an object down to its very atoms and reassembling the object in another location. The government sees this as the ultimate way to move troops around the world instantly, among other uses. I have been interested because of promising related research, which has suggested the theoretical ability to move atoms through time if they are adequately energized and electronically nudged in the right direction.

A Breakthrough

My big break came about a year ago when I somewhat successfully moved a toy wooden block from one side of my lab to the other using A.L.T. I say somewhat, because the first time, the "Y" on the block ended up more like an "X". Subsequent adjustments in the apparatus seem to have corrected this problem.

I won't go into a lot of technical detail, for two reasons. One is that regardless of how much you understand of the science that is known in your day, you have absolutely no way of comprehending the advancements that have been made since then. We can do things now with computers that no one back then even imagined, not even H.G. Wells, himself. The second is that I don't know for sure where these documents are going to end up, and I don't want to give anybody else a head start on what I have worked so hard to attain. In the wrong hands, such a head start could have catastrophic results. So, I will keep the technical details to a minimum, including only enough to give you the general picture and, hopefully, keep it interesting without crossing the line into boring.

Out of the Lab

Moving a toy block across the lab is a long way from moving a person across the same space. I know there are still subtle differences in the reassembled block; some are major enough to be visible. The same differences in reassembling a human being might mean the difference between life and death. So, for the time being, I am content to perfect the technique on inanimate objects.

My next break came about six months ago when I used a device called a laser beam to precisely focus energy in a manner that duplicated the theoretical electronic nudge I referred to above. Unfortunately, I lost my wooden block. It went back to some unknown point in the past.

My First Time Travel Successes

Once I had evidence that the technique was working, I experimented sending objects backward in time in locations that I thought would be unobtrusive. I used old photographs from the library to find places that I could identify as being unchanged today, and sent things back, hoping to retrieve them in the same location in the present. Most of the time I used a grassy hill in what is now a park near the lab grounds. The objects I had the best luck with were short carbon rods, which I transported to a few inches below the surface of the ground. (I know I'm flirting with boring here.) By digging up the rods in the present, I was able to use enhanced radioactive carbon dating to measure how long the rods had been buried, and thus calibrate my apparatus. The advantage I had over others using this method of age determination was that I was able to measure the radioactivity of the rods at the start, which should make the method much more accurate than ever before possible. As a result of this calibration, I think I can transport small objects through time to within a few days of my target date. Soon, I hope you will help me verify this.

<u>Writing to You</u>

Once the technique was perfected, I decided to try to communicate with someone in the past. The old library photographs gave me the opportunity I was looking for. The mailbox on the brick wall of the new (in 1913) drug store is still there today in 2003. By transporting a legally stamped envelope to that mailbox on any date between then and now, it could be mailed and delivered to the addressee, virtually anywhere in the world. Finding a current stamp was easy at a local stamp collector's shop. In fact, I got a whole sheet of 1924 stamps, so I hope to correspond with you regularly, if you will cooperate.

I'm really looking forward to hearing from you. I have fond memories of my great grandmother, Molly, who lived until I was ten. She was younger than her years right up to the end, and she was so much fun to visit. She always made me feel like I was the center of her life, and perhaps I was. I remember her reading to me when I couldn't have been older than three or four and her oatmeal raisin cookies were the best. I found out later that they came from an Amish bakery, but I didn't know any better.

Your son Matthew, my grandfather, was another great figure in my upbringing. He taught me to fish, a distraction I still enjoy whenever I get the chance, and I could always count on seeing him sitting in the bleachers at my baseball games. He lived well, until he died in his sleep just last year, a week after our last fishing outing. I miss him a lot, and think of him every day.

I think I have said enough for this first letter. Whether or not you are willing to write back to me, please don't tell anyone about this letter or its contents. I already am meddling with Mother Nature in ways whose consequences I can not know. Changing the events of the past will inevitably change the present, so the less I change of the past, the more likely I am to maintain the present I know.

If you write back to me, please note the date you received this letter, then seal your letter in an envelope addressed to me, with instructions to hold for personal delivery on June 28, 2003. Leave the envelope with the law firm of Garrison and Krebbs, who probably would be happy to know that they are the largest law firm in town in 2003.

I hope to hear from you tomorrow.

Your great grandson,

Nathan

Diary Entry

May 20, 1924 (cont.)

     I stared at the paper for a long time before I reread it. My first reaction of disbelief lingered as I tried to find the overlooked flaw that would expose this fraud. Subconsciously, I didn't want to find it, because if real, this was the most fantastic thing that had ever happened to me. I reached for the worn book on the shelf, and looked inside the cover of The Time Machine, where I found my name, as I knew I would. Could it really be true that my great grandson would some day find the way to cross the barrier that historically had separated the ages? I wanted it to be true, had dreamed of such an occurrence since I was a boy.

     I didn't know how to react, so I didn't react at first. I went on with my daily routine, pretending to put the letter out of my mind. I had read the mail during my lunch break, so I went back to work to try to conduct business as usual. As I approached the front of the store, I stared at the mailbox on the wall, the mailbox where I routinely drop outgoing mail. Was it true that this box was now also receiving mail from the future?

John Ruhl

By evening, I had decided to go along with the ruse (?) and write a return letter.

Chapter 2

Return 1

April 3, 1924

Mr. Nathan Webb
c/o Garrison and Krebbs

Dear Nathan,

On the chance that I am indeed involved in a legitimate scientific expedition in time, I am responding to your letter, which I received today, April 3, 1924. The mailbox is emptied each evening, so your letter arrived in the box between 5:00 PM April 1 and 5:00 PM April 2.

I must confess to a lingering skepticism, as I am sure you expected. If I had not fantasized so many times about being able to travel through time, I would have dismissed your letter immediately. The fact is, I want this to be true. I want to correspond with someone who does not yet exist. The fact that you are of my own flesh and blood adds even another dimension to the drama. The brief glimpses you have shared about the futures of my wife and son have given me a comfort that is difficult to explain. I suppose it's the reassurance that they will live long and happy lives. So, yes, I will cooperate with you. I will honor your request for secrecy, an easy thing to do when to do otherwise would be to invite sneers suggesting lunacy.

It's hard to know where to begin so I'll tell you a little about me and a typical day in my life, then we'll see where that leads us.

You have an advantage over me, since history has been written to familiarize you with my era and my life. I'll apologize in advance if I bore you too much with details you already know. Everything I know about 2003 is pure speculation on my part and on the part of those writers who have ventured guesses of their own in print. I'm probably most curious about the technological advances you alluded to in your letter.

I was born in 1890 on a farm a few miles east of Nappanee. My father never liked farming, so he moved my family into town in 1895 and bought a grocery store just off the main intersection of Main and Market Streets. His brothers carried on with the farming, and the whole family still lives within a few miles of here. Few of them have been more than twenty miles from home, except for the year some of us spent in Europe during the World War. Fortunately, we all came home from that trip.

We moved from the farm into a house on Main Street, as you know, just two blocks north of the grocery store. I went to grade school and high school a block north of our house, then to Purdue University for a chemistry degree, finishing up my pharmacy degree at Butler in Indianapolis in 1914. I worked for another pharmacist in town until my brief stint in the army during the war, then got a chance to own my own store when I got back. It's right on the southeast corner of Main and Market and next door to my father's grocery, both of us in the new Dietrich building.

I married my high school sweetheart, Molly, when I got back from the war. We had courted off and on since high school, but being away from her in Europe, under dreadful and frightening living conditions changed my perspective of our relationship. I proposed to her the week I got back, and it's the smartest thing I've ever done. Matthew was born in 1919 and is our pride and joy. Our life went from great to greater when he arrived.

I'm lucky to have a best friend whom I've known nearly all my life. We were neighbors after my family moved to town, we grew up together, and now we live in the houses we grew up in and are still neighbors. Hiram married Mary Ellen as soon as he graduated from college, and the four of us have done everything together ever since.

I've recently been diagnosed with terminal cancer. The doctors have told me it's a relatively painless variety, as cancers go, but have given me little hope of surviving it. Molly has been unbelievably supportive, as are Hiram and Mary Ellen. We're trying to live our lives normally, although it's not really possible to do so. Matthew doesn't know yet, and we'll probably hold off telling him as long as we can.

I don't want to dwell on my illness, so let's get on with the program here.

My day usually starts at about 6:00 A.M, when the alarm clock rattles on the dresser by the bed. Getting up is not so difficult as spring sets in, but just a couple months ago was a different story. In the winter, the fire in the furnace has long since burned out by 6:00 o'clock. Getting out of bed each morning is a decision between staying under a comforter that provides at least moderate warmth and going downstairs to rekindle the coal fire that will return real warmth to the house and my bones. The thought of a blazing furnace always wins out eventually, and I drag myself out of bed and down to the basement.

The furnace itself is somewhat of a symbol of my moderate affluence. Most of the homes in town still are heated by potbelly stoves, which burn coal or wood. The obvious benefit of the furnace is that it heats the whole house pretty well, not just the room where the stove is situated. Even the upstairs bedrooms are acceptably warm, as long as the fire is going anyway, thanks to the flow-through registers in the first floor ceilings.

From as far back in my childhood as I can remember, the creak of the cast iron door hinges, first on the stove, now on the furnace, has signaled the start of a new winter day. The new furnace came with a long handled pincer-like tool for removing clinkers from the firebox. I have to remove about half a bucket each morning. The street department uses them to pave the alleys and some of the fringe area streets that haven't yet been bricked.

If I'm lucky, starting the fire can be as simple as stirring up the still-glowing embers and shoveling in some coal. More often than not, though, I have to wad up a few sheets of newspaper, cover the pile with a scoop of coal, strike a match to the paper, then add more coal as the blaze grows. This ritual occupies about the first ten minutes or so of every winter day. It's something I don't miss at all in the summer.

By the time I get back up to the kitchen, Mrs. Webb has completed her similar ritual with the cook stove and the coffeepot usually has started to percolate. Molly has had her eyes on an electric stove in the Sears catalog for some time now. I've ordered one for her birthday. Hopefully, it will get here in time. The house will have to be rewired to use it, but with all the electrical devices Thomas Edison has come up with, it's time we accepted the fact that we are now living in the twentieth century. The few light bulbs we now have in the house are undoubtedly just a glimpse of the conveniences we will see in the next few years. I suspect you have always taken most of them for granted in your lifetime, just as I don't fully appreciate such conveniences as having a bin full of coal instead of having to split wood to keep the house warm. How quickly we become accustomed to these mundane luxuries.

Cream for my coffee comes from the icebox, thanks to the milkman who stops by twice a week and the iceman who does likewise. Gone are the days of my father's childhood when fresh milk came from the cow! I say this in jest, because I much prefer the convenience of living in town. Like my father, I wasn't born to be a farmer.

Back to breakfast, which today is pretty much the same as every other day, two eggs, fried potatoes, and pork side meat. Recently, Molly added toasted bread to the menu when she got her new toaster from the Sears catalog. I suspect Thomas Edison has enjoyed toast for quite a few years, but it's still a novelty in our household. Making the toast is still as much fun as eating it. You just put the piece of bread on the side rack, swing the door up to close it, plug in the cord, wait a minute, flop down the door, which causes the bread to slide down, and close the door again, which causes the now flipped over slice to toast on the other side. What a marvelous gadget. I hope you don't tell me that toast has been replaced with bread capsules or some such futuristic alternative.

After breakfast, it's a short walk up town to the pharmacy, which I open at about 8:00. It doesn't take long for the regular crowd to start wandering in. They are mostly old farmers who have started slowing down as their sons have taken over most of the farming. These guys do their morning chores before the sun comes up, then meander into town to catch up on the latest news from the grapevine. At about

9:00 o'clock, the Chicago paper arrives by train, and they have digested all of it they care to by 10:00, by which time most of them have returned to help their sons on the farm. This ritual is repeated every weekday, but the Saturday morning shopping crowd puts a damper on it until Monday.

I used to leave the store closed on Sundays, but more often than not, somebody's kid had a fever or some other emergency ailment, and I opened up to get them medicine. This happened often enough that I finally gave up and now open up regularly for a few hours on Sunday morning. Somehow, most people feel they can survive from Sunday afternoon or evening until Monday morning without imposing on me to open the store for them, so I seldom get bothered anymore. I enjoy Sunday afternoons, especially after the meal that Molly always fixes for Sunday dinner. After eating twice as much fried chicken or pot roast and mashed potatoes and gravy as I need, I must confess to napping away an hour or so of my afternoon off.

Occasionally we will have the preacher's family over for Sunday dinner, during which time I have to endure the good-natured, but perpetual ribbing from him about how long it's been since he's seen me in church on Sunday morning. It really is good-natured, though, because I had opened up the store for his wife more than once when their kids were sick.

Sunday night supper usually doesn't happen. Popcorn is the meal of choice, and we devour it by the dishpan full while we play checkers or cards or just read by the fire (not by fire light, we do have electric lights! Abraham Lincoln lived and died a long time ago, even from my perspective.). In the summertime, obviously, we forego the fire and spend a lot of time outdoors. We seldom forego the popcorn, however.

On a related subject, you might be interested in where I get the popcorn. Several hundred Amish families populate the community around Nappanee. I doubt if they still exist in 2003, but you obviously have heard of them, since you mentioned cookies from an Amish bakery from your childhood memories. They are a group of people of German descent who live a very simple and devout life, mostly farming, who will have nothing to do with progress. They are unyielding in their religious convictions and look upon modern conveniences as tools of the devil. The adult married men are not allowed to shave, and the women wear bonnets and drab-colored long dresses. Anyway, about five miles south of town, lives an old

Amish man named Eli, who brings his horse and buggy into town every few months and barters for the few goods that he can't produce for himself. Several of the Sunday dinners I mentioned have included Eli's chickens, traded for sulfur or saltpeter or whatever he happened to need at the time.

One of the items I am happiest to get from Eli is his popcorn. The first time I tried it was about five years ago, and since then I have increased my consumption every year until now we have a verbal agreement that I get virtually his whole popcorn crop. If he doesn't need any supplies, I buy the difference with cash. I've started giving ten-pound bags of it as Christmas presents.

I was at Eli's house once as he was preparing the last of a shipment for me. He worked in his basement, first husking the ears, then tediously cutting out any bad spots with his pocketknife. The ears themselves are smaller than I expected, less than half the size of normal field corn. To shell the corn, he then half-filled a gunnysack with the tiny ears and banged the bag against the stone walls of the cellar. This got much of the kernels from the ears and loosened the rest enough to remove easily by hand. When he had a bucket or two full of kernels, he carried them outside and poured them back and forth from bucket to bucket, while the wind separated the chaff from the kernels. He then filled gunny sacks, twenty-five pounds to the bag and tied them shut with a piece of twine. It seemed like a lot of work for a product he sells for two cents a pound.

Anyway, popcorn is the Sunday night ritual, and occasionally any other night of the week. Molly or I fire up the stove, pull out the popper, and pop a dishpan full. The popper is a story in itself. My mother used to use a skillet with a lid, as did her mother before her. We ran across our current popper when a traveling salesman passed through town about five years ago, peddling all kinds of useless contraptions. I was enamored with the corn popper as soon as I heard him describe it. It's so simple; I'm surprised everyone doesn't have one. It's a deep pan made of light gauge black sheet metal, with a red wooden handle and a lid with a stirring blade poking through it. The stirring blade has a knob handle of its own, which you turn as the corn begins to pop. Stirring is a lot easier than shaking an iron skillet. In a matter of minutes, you can pop two or three batches of corn, filling the dishpan, then melt butter in the popper and drizzle it over the corn. My mouth is watering just thinking about it. Every once in a while,

Molly uses bacon grease instead of lard to pop the corn, and then you don't even need butter.

I'm about at the end of this sheet of paper, as good an excuse as any to sign off. I am very anxious to hear from you again, so I hope all goes well with this delivery over the next seventy-nine years.

Very truly yours,

Josiah

Diary Entry

May 20, 1924 (cont.)

I finished writing my first letter at about midnight, sealed it in an envelope, and addressed it as instructed. The next morning, I left the store for a few minutes at about ten o'clock and walked across the street to Joe Garrison's law office with my envelope in my jacket pocket. Joe and I are contemporaries and have known each other since we were kids. What little legal work I need done, he does. I don't know his partner as well, but how many lawyers should a guy need, anyway?

Joe waved me into his office before his secretary had a chance to go through her usual spiel. He was on the phone but obviously finishing up a conversation that wasn't very confidential. I perused the pictures on his mantle while I waited the minute or two for him to finish his call. There were photographs of last year's softball team on which both of us play with comparable ineptitude. The only reason the two of us aren't benchwarmers is the fact that we don't usually have any extra players. Another picture contained both of our sons at play in Joe's back yard. Looking at that image of my son, my mind wandered enough to wonder what my great grandson would look like. The banging of the receiver on the cradle jarred me back to my purpose in being there.

Joe and I exchanged the normal pleasantries about the Cubs' chances this year and the boys' latest adventure in the woods, then he asked me what was on my mind, since I wasn't a frequent visitor at this time of day. I handed him the envelope, and he read what I had written on it the night before. He asked if there was anything I wanted to tell him about it, and I just asked him if he would mind holding on to it for a few years, since he is my personal attorney. He just laughed and asked if I wanted him to quote me a discounted seventy-nine year rate and stuffed the envelope in a folder. On the tab he wrote "Webb, Nathan

Josiah" and put the folder in a file drawer labeled "U-Z".

The phone rang, and I excused myself and headed back to the store, wondering if this emerging adventure could be real and waiting impatiently for the next letter.

The next two days dragged by more slowly than you can imagine. I was like a child waiting for Christmas to come. When the mailman finally dropped it in the box, I was waiting inside my front door, as I had been on the previous day, having run home for lunch in anticipation of the delivery.

Chapter 3

Letter 2, received April 5, 1924

June 27, 2003

Dear Josiah,

As anxious as you may have been to
receive this second letter, I doubt if you can
even imagine the emotions that swept over me
when I stopped at Garrison and Krebs' this
afternoon and found your letter waiting for me.
My first reaction was disbelief. Getting a
response from you represented the culmination
of about twenty years of work, work filled with
failed attempts and blind alleys, but with just
enough tastes of success to keep me interested
and believing I was on the right track. If I never
again were able to duplicate my mail delivery
to the past, this one response from you would
be enough to last the rest of my life. Thus did
my disbelief turn to satisfaction and that to
impatience to get back to my office and open
your letter.

I walked the few blocks and pondered the events of the past two days. I had stopped at Garrison and Krebs' offices yesterday just prior to sending my first letter to you. As a check, I wanted to know if they were holding anything for delivery to me. They were not. Now today, the same fellow handed me your letter as if he had been holding it for me all along, with no mention of our conversation of the day before. When I asked, he said he had only the one letter. I suspect that if I had gone over there immediately after sending the letter yesterday, he would have told me the letter had been held at their office as long as he had been there, and that he wouldn't have recalled our conversation of earlier in the day. I suspect the history of everything connected with that letter was rewritten at least slightly as soon as I sent it to you yesterday. I will have to devise a method of testing that theory properly.

As I sit here looking across my lab, all of the paraphernalia has suddenly taken on a personality of its own. This jumble of wires, circuit boards, computers, and gizmos has been used to accomplish a substantial part of the unfathomable purpose for which it was designed. A project that has seemed so futuristic to me over the years is suddenly culminating in a successful conclusion, and I am awestruck by this realization. I sit here pondering my success and trying to imagine my next steps, but I have to admit that I am somewhat at a loss for the first time in many years.

It's most helpful that you were specific in telling me when the letter arrived. My estimations based on the carbon rod tests were off by about a month. It's nice to have a benchmark for calibrating my equipment. If I'm lucky and the adjustments work as I expect them to, I should be able to get response letters to you a day or two after you deliver yours.

I'm glad to hear that you're a Cubs fan; apparently a tradition that's carried on through the generations in our family. I remember Sundays at my grandmother's, listening to Cubs games on the car radio while my dad washed the car. We were on the other side of Indiana from Chicago, but the weak signal didn't keep us from hanging on every pitch. I hate to be the one to break the news to you, but nearly three-quarters of a century later, we still haven't won a World Series. And the fans still set attendance records at Wrigley Field. Go figure.

I'm impatient about a lot of aspects of my time travel experiments. One of the more important areas of the tests is the study of the condition of those items that have been transported to learn how they are changed by the disassembly and reassembly process. I am, after all, completely taking these objects apart and putting them back together again. It is only logical to expect some anomalies to occur, although I've reached the point of nearly exact duplication in transporting within the confinement of the lab. I have enclosed with this letter a sheet of paper containing a test pattern, which I would like for you to return to me with your next response. The pattern contains precisely drawn and measured icons, which I will be able to test for variations from the originals. Such testing is necessary before I could consider transporting any objects that are more three-dimensional. My ultimate goal, of course, is to transport myself, but I fear to imagine the result if even a few atoms or molecules are reassembled incorrectly. That trip will have to wait a while until the process is perfected and I have had much more practice. For the moment, communicating by letter is enough of a thrill. I plan to enjoy it until the novelty wears off. I can't imagine that happening anytime soon, but as rapidly as scientific advances have changed our lives during the last half century, and then been accepted as commonplace overnight, I hesitate to predict how I will perceive this adventure even as early as next month.

One example that I think you will have a hard time believing is the fact that we are able to travel around the world now in 2003 about as easily as you can drive from Nappanee to Chicago in 1924. Even more unbelievable than that is the fact that we have been to the moon and back several times! It cost a lot of money, and we didn't find much that was very interesting outside the science community, but it did demonstrate that we can accomplish just about anything we have a mind to. Of course, you already know that since you are reading this letter in the first place.

Space travel was something that I was intrigued with as I was growing up. The space program grew up with me, and I spent hours on end reading newspapers, National Geographic magazine, and anything else I could get my hands on which described the latest exploits of our scientists and astronauts. The first satellite took most of the world by surprise. I couldn't read yet so it's no shock that I didn't have any idea what was going on in this regard, but I shared that trait with a lot of knowledgeable adults. A few years later when men started orbiting the earth, my imagination went wild, and I was hooked on following the space program.

The space program started after the end of World War II (hate to break that to you, also). The US brought a bunch of German scientists over here and used what they knew about designing missiles to develop the rockets that would launch satellites and eventually men into space. The first country to put a man up was Russia, who had become a world power by the 1950's. They, as did we, had an arsenal of nuclear weapons (take my word for it - they are very destructive bombs, capable of wiping out entire cities in minutes). The ability of Russia to use rockets to launch those bombs to any city on the globe instilled fear in the rest of the world. That fear created a political tension that shaped policies for decades. It was called the Cold War and lasted almost to the end of the century.

Russia launched their first person into space in 1961, and the US followed soon thereafter. The 1960's were a remarkable time of technological advances. There was intense competition between Russia and the US to land a man on the moon, which the US did in 1969. In order to accomplish that, technologies had to be invented and developed at break-neck pace. The result is an era in which we have instantaneous communication with any place on the planet. Anyone who cares to have one has a phone in his pocket and a computer on his desk (or in his attaché case or even in his pocket!). Those computers can communicate with one another over a system called the Internet, making much of the information that exists in the world available to everyone instantly. Hocus-pocus? It may sound like it, and even seems so to most of us today.

And now, we can communicate with the past and you with the future. I would like to know more about Nappanee in 1924, partly out of curiosity about my history, but perhaps more importantly to allow my experiment to progress. Please take as many photographs as you can, label them with locations on a map of the town, and put them all in an envelope, as before, to be delivered on June 30, 2003. Include in the photos some views of the inside and outside of the brick carriage house behind your house. I would like to be able to send some larger objects, and the carriage house, which is still there today, should be more accommodating than the mail.

I will close now and await your response.

Your great grandson,

Nathan

Chapter 4

Diary entry

May 20, 1924

After getting the assignment to take photographs, I took the Kodak Brownie around town and did as instructed. I was able to get them developed in a couple days through the drug store. I found a great map of Nappanee, and labeled it, the photos and some post cards and stuck them all in a big envelope, along with my return letter and the test pattern page that Nathan had sent. I left the envelope with Joe Garrison, who put it in the drawer with the first letter.

Return 2

April 10, 1924

Dear Nathan,

No World Series championship for the Cubs for almost a century? Tell me you're kidding about that. It was bad enough always hoping for a winning season next year, but to know now that they'll be losing every year takes a lot of the fun out of baseball. You'd think I'd be used to this by now, but following these Cubs is an emotional roller coaster ride. Just when you think they're finally going to be winners, somehow they find a way to let you down hard.

Enclosed are the photos you asked for and a 1915 map of town. A couple residential neighborhoods have been added since then, but what is shown is pretty accurate. In addition to the photos, I found several picture post cards, which are really current and show the town better than do my amateur photographs. I've tried to add enough descriptions so you'll know where the photos were taken. One of the post cards even shows our house and another the building that contains the drug store, also known as the C.H. Dietrich building.

Nappanee itself is a nice town to have grown up in and to raise kids in. It started in 1865 as the town of Locke on a site about two miles north of here but was moved in 1874 when the B&O railroad came through. They actually moved some of the Locke buildings across frozen fields to take advantage of the prime location near the new train station. It's amazing how the B&O reshaped the northern Indiana countryside when it was completed in December of 1874. Towns sprung up overnight from what had previously been cornfields and prairie. Just west of here are Bremen, LaPaz and Teegarden, as examples. Almost as quickly as the railroads created these towns, however, automobiles and the roads that were built to accommodate them sealed the same towns' fate. The roads were laid out for the most part on a grid, following north-south and east-west lines, unlike the railroads, which were built along straight lines between major cities and towns. As a result, many of the towns along the railroads ended up without major highways near them and stopped growing, while those on the highways thrived. Teegarden, which I mentioned previously, is one of those bypassed by the highways and likely will never get any bigger than its present population of about 150. Talk about sleepy.

Nappanee was one of the fortunate ones. Two blocks north of the railroad station, two highways cross at the main intersection in town. One is US 6 (Market Street), which cuts across northern Indiana and south of Chicago. The other, Indiana 19 (which is Main Street, and I live at 301 N. Main, as do you, unless the numbers or names have changed in the meantime), goes to Elkhart north of here and, until recently, not much of anywhere to the south. I say that because a few years ago the Lincoln Highway was completed, running across the continent from New York City to San Francisco. It crosses northern Indiana and passes us about ten miles south of here, so I guess you could say Nappanee has convenient access to New York and San Francisco, perhaps a bit of a stretch.

Nappanee has grown a lot since my family moved here in 1895, but it's still a peaceful country town of about 3000 residents and surrounded by farms of various sizes, about half of which are Amish. The school is a block north of my house on Main, and is second only to the dozen or so churches in town as the social meeting place of the community. Friday night high school basketball games are what we live for in the winter.

Probably because of the Amish and the conservative religious heritage of the founders, before Prohibition Nappanee was home to only one tavern. That's a ratio of twelve churches to one tavern, a notable benchmark I suspect few towns its size can claim, even in Indiana.

The town was well planned, neatly laid out with amply wide streets that are, for the most part, brick-paved and now lined with mature trees. There are several parks, all with baseball fields and picnic pavilions. Crime is almost non-existent; it's hard to imagine Chicago's gangsters are barely a hundred miles away, although rumor has it that some of them pass through here on the train on their way to gambling weekends at Lake Wawasee, twenty miles to the east off the B&O.

Speaking of Lake Wawasee, it's the home of the Wawasee Amusement Company (Waco), and the Waco Dancing Pavilion is one the area's more popular entertainment establishments. It's shown on one of the postcards. Hiram, Mary Ellen, Molly and I spend many summer days and evenings there, swimming, boating, and fishing during the day, then dancing at night. The women even coaxed Hiram and me into taking ballroom dancing lessons last year. We enjoyed it much more than we let on. The lake is certainly one of my favorite places.

Nappanee has its own amusements, of course, in addition to the high school basketball games. The Auditorium was built in 1899, cater-cornered from the building that now houses my drug store. The Auditorium has been used for everything from vaudeville acts to silent pictures, and recently moving pictures with sound. We get visitors from miles away, because it's the best facility of its kind this side of Elkhart and South Bend.

Most recently, we've been home to Chautauqua meetings during the past few summers. In case you haven't heard of it, the purpose of the Chautauqua movement is to provide instruction in Sunday school organization and Bible study while involving recreation and special lectures. The meetings have been very popular here. Molly and the other ladies in the church women's society have been very active participants in these meetings, which first were held in big tents, much like a traveling circus, but without the elephants. Last year, we built a pavilion in West Side Park, largely with the intention of using it for Chautauqua. It was finished just in time, but the event was a money-losing proposition, to the tune of $250, so there's talk of not having it this summer. I hope the rumor is wrong, because the town really gets up for such things. Besides, it's good for my business.

I think your idea about using the carriage house, now the garage, to send and receive things between us would be a good one. There's plenty of space in there, and it would be easy to build a concealed closet-sized room that could be locked and not have to worry about it being disturbed over the years. I've included a couple photos of the interior. If you decide to use it, let me know what size area you need, and I'll get going on it. I'll sign off for now.

Josiah

P.S. I couldn't resist finishing the roll of film with a couple pictures of my family and friends. You may recognize Molly and maybe even Matthew, though I doubt there's much resemblance between a five-year-old and the grandfather you knew. The other picture is of Hiram and Mary Ellen, the dear friends I told you about.

Chapter 5

Diary entry

May 22, 1924

Friday was a long day. It's a fairly busy day at the drug store, payday and all, and I tire quickly these days. Anticipation of another letter took a little of the edge off, but also made the day go by more slowly. An empty mailbox awaited me when I got home that evening. I had better luck Saturday when I walked home for lunch. Hal, the mailman, was just leaving the porch when I walked up the stairs. Hal and Marietta have been good friends of ours since grade school, so we exchanged a few pleasantries and he was on his way.

There were not one, but two envelopes, similar to the first two. I tore open one of them.

Letter 3, received April 12, 1924

June 29, 2003

Dear Josiah,

Thanks for the map and pictures. I'm glad you added the personal photos. There was no mistaking Molly; she aged gracefully over the next fifty years. Matthew, on the other hand, wasn't as easy to identify. Believe it or not, I can see family resemblance between your friend Hiram and his great grandsons, who live in town today. It's very easy to recognize many of the buildings; many of them have changed very little since then. The drugstore building and your house look almost the same today as they did in 1924. The street scenes show the biggest changes, although not as much in Nappanee as in most modern towns and cities. The cars are a lot different today, but horses and buggies still frequent the downtown, and there are still designated parking spaces for them along the streets and in the parking lots. The Amish people have adapted well to changes in others, but have maintained their own culture remarkably, changing their own lifestyle as little as possible over the past couple centuries.

I would like to send you photographs of the way things are today, but after careful consideration have decided against it. I don't want to take the chance that something I send might cause a change in the way your future and my past play out. As it is, I worry every time I send a letter to you that I'll look down and find I'm a girl. So far, so good.

The test pattern you sent back was interesting. As I told you, my technique involves disassembling and reassembling objects right down to the atomic level, and I need to monitor closely the reassembly process to be sure that the result duplicates the original. Transporting living things won't be possible until I can be sure that no structural changes are taking place during the process. The test pattern sheet did show some small variations from what I started with, so I will continue to refine my technique in hopes of reliably eliminating such variations. I have already made some improvements; the first carbon rods I mentioned earlier that I used to calibrate the time shift apparatus showed some deformities when I dug them up. I eliminated that specific problem, but apparently have a few remaining to fix.

I enjoyed your comments about the towns that have grown up along the railroad, and in fact spent four years of my youth in Teegarden. You were right on the money about its population - still 150 today. But it was a nice place to be a boy, and many of my scientific inspirations started out as daydreams there. I can't tell you how many hours I spent sitting in the yard with my back against a tree watching my box kite flying above the field. I made this contraption once that climbed up the string, pulled by a parachute. When it got to the kite, the parachute released and floated back to the ground. It was a fun device, but the problem was that when the parachute was released, it would keep going downwind, which meant it always ended up at least twice as far away as the kite. This isn't a big problem, except I often tried to see how far away I could get the kite.

One particularly blustery afternoon, I kept adding balls of string until the weight of the string made the string almost drag on the ground. By that time I had over a mile of string let out. I clipped the parachute device on the string and let it rip. I watched it with binoculars for as long as I could see it after it was released. I don't know how far it went, because I didn't bother to chase it, but I'm sure it ended up several miles away. It might still be going for all I know.

The fun didn't end there, though. When I decided to reel in the kite, I started winding the reel I had made from a couple pieces of broom handle and some plywood scraps. I already told you the wind was strong, so as I wound in the taut string, eventually it was so tight it snapped one of the broom handles. I was by myself and wasn't willing to sacrifice either string or kite, so I spent over an hour getting the kite reeled in. That personal long distance kite record lives to this day, because it was the last time I ever wanted to work at it that hard.

Teegarden was a great place for my hobbies to develop. I was in Boy Scouts and got an idea at a Jamboree one winter. A Jamboree is a get-together in an exhibit hall or gym where scout troops from the region get a chance to show off what they have learned or share their latest projects. One of the scout troops had a chemistry demonstration at their booth and was making hydrogen by electrolysis of water in a test tube, then igniting it with a match, resulting in a loud "pop". At one point, they decided to make a really loud bang and used a large beaker instead of a test tube. They made a bang all right and blew shards of the exploded beaker all over the room. We're lucky nobody got hurt then or during any of our other hair-brained escapades.

Back to my story – I knew from something I read somewhere that you could also make hydrogen by mixing muriatic acid and zinc, so I started filling balloons with hydrogen by mixing the concoction in a pop bottle capped by a balloon. The hydrogen filled the balloon, which would float in the air when the neck was tied off. I tied self-addressed notes to the balloons, and released them into the air, with daydreams of getting responses from the other side of the ocean. While that never happened, I did get letters from Ohio and West Virginia, both from farmers who found the balloons in their fields. As it turns out, the hydrogen would leak from the balloons fast enough that they would only stay inflated about 12 hours (at least when tested in my room), so they didn't have time to get across the ocean before they came down.

One more Teegarden story, then I'll move on. This one also stems from my Boy Scout days. I got a magazine called "Boys Life" through scouts and always read it cover to cover. My sister would add that I usually read it in the bathroom. By the way, it was from Boys Life that I first got interested in time travel. Occasionally there would be a story about a Boy Scout troop that had adventures in their time machine, and I always looked for those stories first, although they appeared much less frequently than I would have preferred.

One month, I responded to an ad from the classifieds in the back of Boys Life and ordered a telescope for $3.98. That wasn't a lot of money in 1970 unless you saved it a nickel or dime at a time, which I did. Starting a few days after I put the order in the mail, every afternoon I would watch for the mail bag to be thrown from the passing train, walk to the post office and wait impatiently while the postmaster sorted the mail into the boxes. Ours was Box 5. I probably did that every day for two weeks. One day, I didn't go, for whatever reason. At 5:00 PM, our phone rang. The postmaster told my mother that a package had arrived for me, and if I would come right away, she would stay open long enough for me to get there. One of the advantages of living in a town of 150 people, and I'll never forget that considerate act.

The telescope turned out to be worth about what I paid for it, three telescoping cardboard tubes with cheap lenses and no mount, but it got me started on a hobby that I still enjoy today. I've gone through a few telescopes since then, but I still have that one, and it holds a special place in my memory banks.

Back to the issue at hand. I am convinced that the garage would be a good place to start transporting items back and forth. I have a few ideas about building a portable enclosure that I could send backward in time and then retrieve it by a preprogrammed procedure. I don't know how to do it in a self-powered vehicle like H.G. Wells imagined it, but I think I could control it from my lab in the year 2003. I don't know how much room this enclosure will occupy, so I will start experimenting with the idea now and when I am successful, I will send you another letter to arrive at the same time as this one, with specific dimensions I will need in the room you build. If you haven't received the second letter yet, it should arrive shortly.

Until then, I remain your humble great-grandson,

Nathan

Diary entry

May 22, 1924 (cont.)

I had many things I wanted to say to my great-grandson, but first I opened the other letter and read on....

Letter 4, received April 12, 1924

November 12, 2003

Dear Josiah,

Hopefully, you have received another letter from me written on June 29, but if you haven't, the contents of the letter you are reading now will make more sense after you have read the other.

I have spent the past five months developing a cage-like enclosure in which I hope to transport objects back to the past and retrieve them to the present. As we have discussed before, you will need to build a small room in your garage, dedicated to this use. It is imperative that you build the room exactly as I have instructed to insure that nothing is in the room during transport. I shudder to think what two objects trying to occupy the same space would look like.

I have included a sketch to make your job a little easier and to eliminate any confusion about the necessary design. You will observe that the room is built in two parts. The main section is like an empty closet, six feet wide, four feet deep and eight feet tall, just tall enough to fit under the rafters. Behind the back wall is an eighteen-inch deep cavity, which will house a companion chamber containing the electronic apparatus necessary to retrieve the main chamber from the past back to the present. The electronics are very sensitive and must be inaccessible to avoid tampering or accidental damage. Thus, the cavity is sealed with solid walls and ceiling.

Let me know when you finish the construction and I will give you additional instructions and a schedule for the christening.

Nathan

Chapter 6

Diary entry

May 23, 1924

Molly had wanted me to clean out the garage, so Sunday afternoon I did it. Hiram dropped over and helped for a while, and by evening, it looked like a different place. Monday I had the lumber yard deliver the materials I needed for my project, and Monday evening I started in earnest building the new storage closet I suddenly found a need for. The urgency of this closet baffled Molly, but I think she was happy to see me busy and didn't object.

My Uncle Biney (J. Byron Miller, actually, and not really my uncle but a family friend) was a carpenter, and I learned enough helping him as a child to get me through a lifetime of easy projects such as this one. By the weekend, I had turned the key and locked the closet door, ready for the next phase of this unlikely adventure.

Return 3

April 21, 1924

Dear Nathan,

The room is finished, built exactly as you instructed. I have enclosed a few photographs, including one showing the studs before I attached the plywood wall over the cavity. I was lucky to get the plywood on short notice; it's still a bit of a novelty item and not kept in stock like solid lumber is. I used brass screws instead of nails for the walls and ceiling of the cavity to eliminate any possibility of exposed nails. I'll take your word that this detail could be significant in preventing interference to the electronics, but then you're the expert on this hocus-pocus. I'm just the carpenter.

Enclosed you'll find something you didn't ask for, but which will come in handy. It's a key to the closet door.

I'm ready for Phase 2. Let's get this show on the road.

Josiah

Diary entry

May 23, 1924 (cont.)

Joe Garrison didn't even crack a joke that morning when I gave him the third letter.

Chapter 7

Diary entry

May 23, 1924 (cont.)

   The previous week's work had worn me out, and I was ready to step away from the project for a couple days to get the rest of my life back on schedule. Nathan cooperated and I didn't get another letter from him until Wednesday, by which time I was chomping at the bit again.

Letter 5, received April 23, 1924

July 7, 2003

Dear Josiah,

   What an awesome new dimension time is turning out to be. Despite my having devoted much of my life to learning about it, I marvel at its intricacies every time I experience a new facet. As soon as I sent the letter of June 29, in which I told you I would need you to build the garage closet, I checked the garage, and the new room was there, as if it had been there all along. I don't even know the size I will need yet, but obviously I will be giving you the size in a future letter, which you apparently have received already. This is becoming confusing to me, and I'm supposed to be in charge here. But, oh what fun.

I will be sending my next letter directly to the closet on April 25. Having used the mailbox for all letters thus far, I still can only estimate the time of day the transport will happen, so it's important to keep the closet empty for the whole day. Over the course of the next few deliveries, I may be able to pin the arrival time down to within an hour or so, but I don't have the feedback from you yet to be that accurate. In the interest of safety first, please follow these few precautions to the letter.

1. In the exact center of the floor, paint a circle, about a foot in diameter.
2. On the evening of April 24, thoroughly clean the closet.
3. Lock the door when you're finished and don't open it again until the morning of April 26.
4. Leave your next letter with Garrison and Krebs, telling me you're ready.

5. As soon as you open the door on the 26th, take some photos of the floor before disturbing it. A photo from directly overhead would be good.
6. When you have the photos developed, send them to me via Garrison and Krebs and lock the door again until further instruction.

As soon as I send this letter, I'll run over to Garrison and Krebs' office to pick up your reply. I also am anxious to get this show on the road.

Nathan

Chapter 8

Diary entry

May 23, 1924 (cont.)

The reality of my garage closet being used as a portal from the future was more than a little unnerving. There was something more detached about the mailman bringing the letters. "Sometime else" isn't that much different from "somewhere else" since both are "away from here". Receiving something from the year 2003 directly in my garage, however, seemed a more direct violation of my sense of the way things are, always have been and always will be. I'm probably not making sense; you had to be there.

Again, I followed my instructions, painted the circle on the floor, cleaned and locked the closet and sent my next letter.

Return 4

April 24, 1924

Dear Nathan,

     The garage closet is ready for use, prepared according to your directions. The anticipation is growing as we start Phase 2 of this adventure. I can't tell you how anxious I am to open that door the day after tomorrow. I wish you luck as you make whatever changes you have to make in your equipment and procedures.

Josiah

Chapter 9

Diary entry

May 24, 1924

How I got through the long day of April 25th I'll never know. The minutes dragged by, in spite of the fact that it was a Friday, and the store was particularly busy. I'm reminded of similar feelings on Christmas Eve as a boy, after I was supposed to be asleep, but my mind refusing to shut down, thinking instead of the toys that would be under the tree. Those nights went by so slowly, until I was a little older and learned to occupy my mind with jigsaw puzzles and adventure books. Now I was relying on encounters with Eli (remember Eli the popcorn man?) and the other drug store customers to make the time pass.

When I got home that evening, it was Christmas Eve in April. I tried to read, but my mind wandered. Only the fatigue of the workday, compounded by my progressing illness, allowed me to fall asleep that night.

I awoke early and went straight to the garage. Everything appeared to be as I had left it. I put the key in the lock and opened the closet door. I didn't notice it immediately in the early dawn shadows, but there on the floor, slightly askew on the painted circle, was a hinged metal box, maybe ten inches long, six inches wide, and a couple inches deep. Somehow I remembered to take some pictures of it before I picked it up and carried it into the house. Although I don't specifically remember it, I suspect my hands were trembling as I fumbled with the latch and opened the box. Inside were a few small trinkets and a familiar looking envelope, this time without stamp and postmark.

Letter 6, received April 26, 1924

July 8, 2003

Dear Josiah,

If you are reading this, the new delivery method worked, and I look forward to your confirmation of such. To get to this point required moving much of my apparatus from the lab to the garage, a move that went smoothly enough that I didn't have to spin my wheels much. After minor calibration, I was ready to go. In the box along with this letter you should have found a few small items that I'm using to study how well the reassembly process is working. They are all souvenir trinkets either from my own travels or which have been in the family for a while. There's a Liberty Bell, a letter opener from Washington, D.C., and a paperweight from the Chicago World's Fair. Please send them back with your confirmation letter, again via Garrison and Krebs.

In case it isn't obvious to you why I'm continuing to use Garrison and Krebs instead of you just sending the letters directly in the closet, if we were to use the closet for forward moving deliveries, I'm afraid the closet would get crowded. Like I've mentioned to you before, I'm concerned about multiple objects trying to occupy the same space and don't want to send an object to you that might reassemble within the confines of an object already occupying the same space. I have avoided that problem thus far by transporting the letters into the top of the mailbox, where they reassemble then drop to the top of whatever mail, if any, is already in the box. Now we're entering a new arena, with increased possibility of interference between new and existing objects in the garage closet, so I want to limit the closet's use to deliveries from me to you for the time being.

I'll make my next delivery on April 27, so go through the same routine again, cleaning and locking the closet the evening of April 26, then leaving the room locked until the morning of the 28th.

All the best,

Nathan

Chapter 10

Diary entry

May 24, 1924 (cont.)

And so Phase 2 began. Nathan did as he had promised and made a delivery on April 27 and about every two days for the next month. He sent all kinds of small objects, most of which he wanted me to send back for him to study. Joe Garrison moved my packages into their own drawer in his filing cabinet when they outgrew the folder he had put them in originally. Nathan shared with me some of the science behind his invention and told me the reasons he was sending the objects he was sending, but the frequency of the deliveries and the amount of my time that was occupied by my part of the experiments made it difficult for me to keep up with recording the events in this diary.

My health is failing. The past month has taken its toll. I told Nathan in my last letter that I needed a few days off to catch up, and he has not made a delivery now since May

*19, with the next one scheduled for tomorrow,
and a special delivery it should be.*

Letter 15, received May 19, 1924

October 14, 2003

Dear Josiah,

I fully understand your request for some time off. I have been pushing you very hard over the past month and should have had the foresight to consider your health when setting my schedule. After all, I have the entire future over which to do my work; there's no need to compress the work at your end into an unreasonable timeframe. That being said, I will delay my next delivery until May 25 unless I hear differently from you.

I picked the 25th because it's a Sunday, and this package will require a little more attention than the others have. I'm going to send a dog, so you will need to listen periodically throughout the day, so you will be able to release him from the confinement of the closet within a reasonable time after he arrives. No reason to traumatize him any more than he will have been already just making the trip. I have done this successfully in the lab without the time travel and am confident that it will be a humane thing to do. I have no reason to believe that the dog will suffer any pain whatsoever; the laboratory animals have all behaved in a very docile manner after Atomic Level Transport, seemingly unchanged from their previous states.

The dog I'll be sending is named Spot. I rescued him from the pound a couple weeks ago in anticipation of this experiment. Please be prepared to take photos and send me your observations after he arrives next week.

Nathan

Chapter 11

Diary entry

May 25, 1924

I write this with a new friend by my side. He's the friendliest mixed-breed I have ever seen. He's pure white, with a tail and tongue that never stop moving. My guess is that he's less than a year old, because he's full of puppy playfulness. His body shape is similar to a Lab, but he's much smaller than a Lab and has very short hair.

I had checked the garage closet this morning before I left to open the drug store, and hadn't heard a sound. By the time I got home, shortly after noon, I could hear whimpering and opened the door to find a cage with Spot inside. He was a little timid at first, as was I with a strange animal, but we both warmed up to one another pretty quickly. I can't get over how quickly Molly agreed to have a dog in the house. She has resisted Matthew's begging for a pet in the past, but today showed no sign of disagreement and in a matter of minutes was playing with Spot with as much enthusiasm as Matthew was.

I took a few photos throughout the afternoon. I'll get them developed in the morning and send them back to Nathan.

Return 15

May 26, 1924

Dear Nathan,

Your latest experiment is an unqualified success. Spot (and I do appreciate your sense of humor in naming him that) is a delightful companion, an opinion shared by my son and wife. He is curled up beside me as I write this, a victim of a very long day of travel and playing in his new surroundings. If he suffered any ill effects from his journey, they are not apparent. He's a playful pup, and one I'm happy to have around. I suspect you were sad to see him go. Photographs are enclosed.

Josiah

Letter received May 28, 1924

November 4, 2003

Dear Josiah,

I'm happy that Spot survived the perilous journey in apparent good health, but as you can see by the photos I took of him before I sent him to you, my sense of humor isn't that good. I named him Spot because of the big spot around his right eye, and that spot didn't survive the trip. This may seem like a minor problem, but until animals can be sent without any observed changes, it certainly won't be safe for a human to make the trip. A very small anomaly in the way the brain is reassembled, for instance, could make a dramatic change in the person's personality or even their ability to function. So, the experiment was not an unqualified success, but I have made some adjustments to the apparatus over the past two weeks and hope that I have corrected the problem. To test the modifications, I will be sending a multicolor guinea pig on May 30. Take plenty of photos, and send them back. If all has gone well, then we will move into the next phase.

I am about finished on the hardware that will allow direct transport back to me. I'll discuss it in the next letter.

Nathan

Chapter 12

Diary entry

May 30, 1924

    Had anyone told me, as recently as a month ago, that I would now be treating as routine this new phenomenon of receiving mail and other stuff from eighty years in the future, I would have called them crazy. Since I am the only one in the present that knows about these comings and goings, I needn't worry about that speculation. Never the less, I am dumbfounded that I have shifted into this mode of not being surprised when a new delivery comes. For crying out loud, none of this can be happening! But it is, and I'm checking the mailbox and opening the garage closet door, more surprised when I don't find anything than when I do.

    Don't get me wrong; I'm enjoying this escapade as much now as I did in the beginning, but I'm so wrapped up in it that it's now second nature to me. So, when I got up this morning, I had breakfast even before checking the garage for the latest arrival. There was no sound behind the door in the morning, nor again at noon, but by evening I heard scratching noises and cautiously opened the door to find a cage and what at first looked like a porcupine. On closer look, it was obviously a guinea pig. Nathan hadn't exaggerated when he said multicolored. This creature had more colors of fur than I had ever seen on an animal. I took several photographs, then took him into the house to join the growing zoo. By the end of the evening he was right at home.

I really wish I could tell Hiram about this project. We have always done such things together in the past, and I feel terrible leaving him out of this. I know he would enjoy the adventure as much as I do, and it would be nice to be able to talk to someone about it.

Letter received May 31, 1924

November 29, 2003

Dear Josiah,

Thanks for sending plenty of photos of the guinea pig. I've compared them all with those that I took and I can't see any differences between them. Hopefully the glitch that caused Spot's problem has been corrected.

I'm ready to move ahead with the next phase of the project and send a retrievable cage on June 4. It will be a tubular framed enclosure, just a box with open sides. I built it in the closet, and it's too big to fit through the door. It's not very impressive to look at. It's just a container enclosing whatever is being transported; the working part will be behind the back wall of the closet. As I told you before, the electronics are very sensitive, and I can't take any chances with accidental abuse, either by humans, animals, or weather.

The first objects I send in the transporter will be inanimate, similar to those I sent to you originally. Once the box arrives, take photographs as usual, then send them to me via Garrison and Krebs. This is where the procedure departs from what has been "ordinary". As soon as you have photographed everything, leave all the items in the transporter box and add something of your own. Lock the closet door, and within twenty-four hours I'll attempt to bring the assembly back to 2003. The electronics will remain in the enclosure behind the wall for use in subsequent transports.

Once I get your photographs at Garrison and Krebs' office, I will compare them with the objects as I sent them and the same objects after they have made the return. If there is any difference, the photos should at least give me a clue whether the changes happened on the trip backward or forward in time.

Until next time,

Nathan

Diary entry

May 31, 1924

Forget anything I said about this becoming routine. Nathan has me on the edge of my seat again, then pacing impatiently waiting for June 4. Fortunately I have doctor's visits and treatments on Monday and Tuesday that will keep me occupied much of the time until Wednesday the 4th.

Diary entry

June 3, 1924

These treatments have taken a lot out of me. I sometimes question whether they are worth the additional discomfort they cause. Between the injections and awful tasting stuff I have to drink, followed by Milk of Magnesia, which settles my stomach some, but not without the inevitable purging of my bowels, I feel much worse after the treatments than I did before. Sorry to be so graphic, but that's my life at the moment. Three things make it worthwhile: my wife and son, for whom I must try to get through this, and my ongoing adventure with my great grandson. Tomorrow should be fun.

Chapter 13

Diary entry

June 4, 1924

Breakfast was the farthest thing from my mind as I rose this morning, partly the aftermath of the previous two days of treatments, but mostly the anticipation of finding something new in the garage. I ignored Nathan's advice not to open the door and inched it open enough to see that there was nothing there before closing it again. Lunchtime was another matter. It was obvious to me as I started opening the door that my wait was over. Not only was there something inside the closet, but it nearly filled the closet completely. As Nathan had described it, the contraption was indeed an open box made of tubular steel, almost as big as the interior of the closet. It had a solid bottom upon which were several objects, obviously chosen because they were readily available, not for their scientific value. There was a quart milk bottle, a small box of nails, a hammer, a shoe, and several other nondescript items. I photographed them, placed on the floor beside them a book about the Titanic, took another photograph of the closet interior, then locked the door to wait again.

Diary entry

June 5, 1924

> *I was more cautious this morning and waited until noon to check the garage. The closet was empty, except for my Titanic book, which lay on the floor. The experiment had been successful enough to get the transporter on its way, but I would have to wait to see if it made it all the way to 2003.*

Letter received June 6, 1924

December 1, 2003

Dear Josiah,

I'm happy to report that the transporter returned within about fifteen minutes of the expected time, all occupants intact. This is a remarkable achievement, more than I hoped to accomplish on the first attempt. There were so

many things that could have gone wrong, so many parts of the apparatus that had not been tested, that I wouldn't have been surprised never to have seen that transporter again. But here it is, and I'm elated to be reporting the success.

I noticed you didn't send anything back in the transporter, other than the items I sent to you, so I compared the contents with the photos you sent via Garrison & Krebbs. I see that there was a book in the transporter before its departure. I assume the transporter left it behind. I'm starting to formulate in my mind the rules of time travel. Before this experiment is over, I hope to record those rules, which I am discovering as we go along. I just hope we don't violate any of them before we understand what they all are. Who knows what will happen if we do?

I have examined all of the items after their trip in the transporter and can find no changes in any of them. I'll send another guinea pig next on June 8. It would be a good idea to feed him and give him a drink of water, and I will retrieve him during the next day.

As long as the deliveries are being retrieved successfully, I will send the transporter every other day, retrieving it on the following day in every case. I'll only send letters by mail if I need to for some unforeseen reason, such as equipment modifications or maintenance, during which time I might want to give you special instructions without the transporter available to deliver them.

I hope you're having as much fun with this project as I am.

Nathan

Diary entry

June 8, 1924

The guinea pig arrived sometime during the morning.

Diary entry

June 9, 1924

The closet was empty by noon today. More treatments this afternoon. I'm very tired.

Diary entry

June 17, 1924

Over the past 9 days, the garage closet has been the temporary home of first the guinea pig, then a dog, a cat, two cats, then a cage containing four rabbits. Nathan made it pretty easy for me by packaging containers with food for the animals, so all I had to add was water. It's good that he did, because I'm getting weaker by the day. I don't think I'll be able to go to work much longer. I'm down to only working in the mornings now, and on the days I get treatments I can't work at all.

My declining health has not made me any less curious, though. I have to confess that it got the best of me this afternoon. Once I was sure the transporter was gone, I went into the closet and removed the screws holding the back wall panel in place and pulled the panel back far enough to see behind it. What I saw was a modest contraption with a few wires and some electrical gizmos visible, all surrounded by a tubular structure much like the transporter I have become familiar with. The tubular box pretty much filled the space available for it.

There was no noise and not a clue from looking at it what it was or how it worked. It was impossible to get a good enough angle to take a picture, so I replaced the panel with the screws and locked the closet door. The last time I felt like this was after going through my father's sock drawer, hoping to find glossy photos like one of my friends had found while snooping in his father's things. I wasn't as successful as he had been, and it was weeks before I was able to sit at the dinner table and not feel that the guilt was showing all over my face.

Return 18

June 17, 1924

Dear Nathan,

The zoo that has passed through my garage closet over the past week has been remarkable entertainment. I assume since they've kept coming that all is going well at your end.

I need to alert you to my deteriorating condition. I don't know how much longer I will be able to keep up with you and your project. I am working less now and may not be able to continue working much longer. With that in mind, I started writing another letter advising you of my demise, to be left with Joe Garrison, with instructions that he date it and put it in the drawer with the others upon my death. As I was writing it, it occurred to me that you know from local and family records when I am going to die, and undoubtedly have known all along, so I didn't finish the letter.

I can't begin to tell you how much this project has meant to me and to thank you adequately for making me a part of it. I feel like I have made an unimaginably significant contribution to science, but more importantly, I appreciate the contact with you, my great grandson, and the glimpses of my family that will survive me.

Josiah

Chapter 14

Diary entry

June 18, 1924

When I checked the garage closet this afternoon, the door was unlocked and standing wide open. I didn't see him at first; it was a sunny day and my eyes hadn't yet adjusted to the shadows inside the garage.

I turned, startled, as he said, "Josiah?"

He was tall, thin, and had long sandy hair, just short of curly, and he was dressed in a contemporary suit that somehow gave the appearance that it was very old.

"Josiah, don't be frightened. I'm Nathan."

Chapter 15

I stared in disbelief, then after an indeterminate time, was greeted with a hug that approached painful. Neither of us said much for the longest time, but then we both started laughing, pounding each other on the back, and mumbling such things as, "I can't believe it" and several variations of the same. After a minute or so, I stood back and looked him over. I thought I could see a family resemblance. Something that I didn't notice right away was his left hand. The ring and little fingers were curled up in a cramped position, with the index and middle fingers curled less tightly, but not appearing to move, never the less. The bent thumb completed the prosthetic-looking hand. He must have noticed me staring at it and put his hand in his pocket.

"Greetings from the year 2003," he said next.

I didn't know how to respond.

"I come in peace." He grinned, and the ice was broken.

I don't remember everything we said, but we spent much of the afternoon sitting in the back yard, talking about family I would never know or that Nathan had only read about. He would be staying one week, after which time the transporter would automatically return to 2003.

Molly arrived home from working at the church rummage sale at about 4:00, and I introduced her to my cousin from Pennsylvania, a story we had concocted to avoid the truth, which we didn't yet know how to deal with. He was in town for a week, staying at the Coppes Hotel while working out some orders at the Coppes kitchen factory.

Molly invited Nathan to have dinner with us, and I walked uptown with him to get a room at the hotel and to help him find some clothes for the coming week. He had brought only the clothes he was wearing, a suit from his grandmother's closet (my son's perhaps?). A quick stop at the clothing store and Nathan was ready for whatever lay ahead. The hotel had plenty of rooms available, so we were back home before dinner was ready.

Dinner conversation was a little awkward at times, partly because of the incredible drama we were participating in, and partly because Molly and my son were not privy to the drama, and talking around the edges of it was difficult. When dessert was finished, we moved to the living room and Matthew quizzed Nathan about Pennsylvania until it was time for Matthew to go to bed. I walked back uptown with Nathan, and we made plans to meet the next day for lunch, after I had put in my half day at the store. Of course, Molly had booked Nathan for dinner every night that he was willing to join us.

We said goodnight, and I walked slowly down Main Street, pondering the events of the day. I was exhausted, but knew that I needed to document the day while it was fresh in my mind. As I finish this entry, I am so tired that I know I will sleep, despite my brain's desire to go over the day event by event.

Chapter 16

Diary entry

June 19, 1924

The morning went by very slowly at the store. I was exhausted from the long day yesterday, and I had other things I would rather have been doing. I told the regulars about my cousin in from Pennsylvania and had to do some tap dancing when I realized one of them was a Coppes kitchen salesman. I managed to skirt the issue, avoiding specific answers to what Nathan was doing in town, and nobody pressed for any more than I offered.

At noon, I walked down the block to the hotel and found Nathan waiting in the lobby. We cut through the alley and went in the back door of Mish's, formerly Mish's Tavern, but these Prohibition days just Mish's, a restaurant frequented at lunchtime by most of the businessmen in town. I've realized lately how much I enjoy these lunchtime gatherings, a group of men, some of whom are friendly rivals, but in more cases just friends catching up on the past day's happenings. It doesn't hurt that the food is good.

Nathan followed me over to my regular table, a long one already partially occupied by a grocer, a jeweler and a clothier with lunch specials in various degrees of completion in front of them. Nathan had met John Hartman yesterday when we bought clothes at John's store, across Main Street from the pharmacy. The other introductions were made, and in minutes we had our own plates of the Thursday meat loaf special. Missing from the table was Ira Dunham, my new business partner, who was taking up the slack of my diminishing work schedule. We usually don't go to lunch at the same time, to insure that a pharmacist is always available. Ira has only been my partner for a couple months. When I realized that my health was not likely to return, I wrote to Ira, originally from Nappanee and then half owner of a drugstore in Union Mills, in hopes that he might be interested in relocating back to a more thriving community. The timing was right; he jumped at the chance and bought half interest. In all likelihood, Ira's brother-in-law Walter Love will buy me out in a few months, and

Webb's Drugstore will be no more. I don't know what the new name will be, but my guess is Dunham & Love.

Nathan turns out to be very personable, and soon was indistinguishable from the regulars, talking about politics and the Cubs, and other subjects I don't recall. He apparently had done his homework, because he didn't once slip in the name of a Cubs player from his era and knew enough of the current players' names and positions to hold up his part of the conversation.

The men started heading back to their jobs at about 1:00, and soon we were the last ones remaining and also left. We walked the two blocks to my house, and after checking in with Molly, went to the garage, peeked in on the transporter in the closet, then backed the '23 Model T into the alley, and started a tour of the little city. Nathan's delight was obvious as he recognized at least three-quarters of the houses and other buildings within six blocks of downtown. He pointed out remodeled features and color changes, but was fascinated by how little had changed until we got to the outskirts of town. His eyes got wide, though, as he described how the town would stretch beyond its current borders with new factories near the railroad, commercial areas along the highways and new residential areas everywhere else.

We drove out into the country, where Nathan observed that farms were smaller than they would be in the future as machines would make it possible for farmers to plant and care for much more acreage. Many of the farm houses and buildings would be replaced by more luxurious homes as people who had jobs in town but wanted the space of the country would move out of town. I suppose it makes sense, but it seems a little ironic that while farmers were changing careers and moving into town where the jobs are, the town people who already have the town jobs would be moving out to the country. The grass is always greener....

I ran out of steam quickly, so we drove back to town, where we found that Molly had baked a couple of cherry pies and oatmeal raisin cookies, both favorites of mine. Baked anything in the summertime is appreciated, because the heat of the oven makes the kitchen pretty warm, but the weather has been moderate this week, and I am the grateful beneficiary. The pies were for supper, but the cookies were fair game. I was pleased to learn that Molly had invited our neighbors, Hiram and Mary Ellen Ruhl, over to eat with us and to meet

Nathan. Hiram has been my best friend for as long as I can remember, and I looked forward to finally making him a part of this adventure, albeit an unknowing participant. Nathan is adamant about not telling the real story to anyone. He is extremely cautious about not changing any more than necessary in his past. It has been obvious a couple times that he is a bit apprehensive about his return trip. Perhaps it's a fear of what he has changed already and how it will effect the environment he will find when he returns.

Nathan, Matthew and I had cookies and milk in the backyard, where Matthew continued to drill Nathan about Pennsylvania. It was delightful watching them interact, the five-year-old grandfather and his forty-something grandson. I would have liked to tell Matthew the whole story, but knew I couldn't. Nathan, on the other hand, knew the whole story and seemingly was enjoying getting to know his grandfather. Eventually Matthew ran off to play with one of his friends, and Nathan and I continued our catching up (or back, as the case may be).

I'm afraid I was less than a gracious host and fell asleep in the chaise lounge somewhere in the middle of a discussion of

Nathan's grade school days, much of it spent at this very house and at the school right down the street. I must have slept nearly two hours and was awakened by my friend Hiram, who was carrying a tub of homemade ice cream, still packed in ice. What a welcome sight. I haven't been able to make ice cream for a couple months now, and Matthew is still a little young to manage the crank himself, so we have done without. I remembered the pie and was elated all over again. Cherry pie a la mode. Does it get any better than this? Well, as it turns out, it does, because while I had been sleeping, Nathan had taken over as chef and was finishing a batch of barbecued pork ribs. I am normally the barbecuer, but was happy to yield to Nathan today. Molly's potato salad and baked beans finished the menu, and we enjoyed a feast, shared around the picnic table in the yard.

By the time we finished the pie and homemade ice cream, it was going on 8:00. Nathan, Hiram and I continued talking for a while sitting in the yard. The two of them had hit it off from the beginning. I continue to be impressed how Nathan has adapted to this era. He is able to talk like a current resident, with no indication that he was just dropped here a couple days ago. I feel proud of him and his accomplishments as I would any offspring, but at the same time feel slightly distanced from him.

I didn't last long in the conversation again. I found myself nodding off, undoubtedly a combination of the long day and my medications. I excused myself, and Nathan and Hiram said goodnight to Molly and walked toward town, probably continuing a discussion of the Cubs or some other subject I missed out on when I fell asleep. I started this diary entry then, but didn't get far, so I finished it in the morning. I have made arrangements with Ira to manage the store without me until Nathan leaves, so hopefully I will have a little more energy than I've had the last two days.

Chapter 17

Diary entry

June 20, 1924

  I slept in this morning. By the time I finished yesterday's diary entry and was ready to leave the house, it was nearly 11:00. Nathan was due to arrive for lunch soon, so I puttered around, catching up on neglected paperwork until he showed up. After a quick bite, we headed south of town to Eli's, so Nathan could experience an authentic Amish farm. We were taking our chances on finding Eli at home. He didn't have a phone, so we couldn't forewarn him of our visit. Fortunately, he was weeding his garden when we drove up to his place.

  Eli is an old bachelor, probably in his sixties, but it's hard to tell. Amish farmers live a hard life, and their weathered bodies and long gray beards make them just look old. I told him Nathan wanted to see how he processed his popcorn, and Eli was happy to oblige. He led us in through the back porch, which was cluttered with tools and small farm implements waiting to be repaired. He stopped long enough at the sink to rinse off some of the garden mud, part of which remained on the pump handle. The house hadn't been cleaned for a while, a fact that didn't seem to bother Eli. We walked through the living room, roughly in the middle of the house and containing a potbellied stove, which provided heat for the whole house in winter. Eli burned wood for fuel and had a stack in the yard that looked adequate for the next two winters.

Off the side of the living room was the stairs to the basement. It had been built for small people, and it was a bit of a squeeze getting down. There was enough light from the windows at the top of the walls that Eli didn't light the oil lamp. He showed Nathan how he prepared and bagged the popcorn as I described in one of my first letters to him. In a few minutes, he knew everything he wanted to know about popcorn, and we backtracked up the stairs and out the back door. We had a tour of his barn and saw his two horses in the small pasture beside it. Eli's needs were simple and apparently he was content with his life and his little piece of the countryside.

During last night's dinner and activities, Nathan noticed my telescope sitting in a corner and commented about it. We are both amateur astronomers, so he was very interested in the telescope and its history. He had told me in an early letter about his interest in the hobby, but looking back at that letter now, it was received when we started discussing building the garage closet and I never followed up telling him that I shared his interest in astronomy.

My first telescope was a Civil War spyglass that I was given by my grandfather. Since it originally didn't have a mount, it was mainly good for looking at craters on the moon. When I was about sixteen, I built a crude mount that was little more than a ball joint on a wooden tripod. That telescope served me well, and with it I saw Halley's Comet up close in 1910 as well as many good views of the planets over the years. Two years ago I saw an ad in Scientific American magazine for a New Jersey telescope manufacturer, W & D Mogey. I sent them the small fortune of $195 and received in return a 3" brass tube refractor, a finder scope, objective cap, three eyepieces, and a diagonal. The scope is mounted on a wood tripod with a cast alt-azimuth mount. It's a beauty and in *fact looks so good that Molly doesn't mind it sitting in the corner of the living room.*

When Nathan saw the Mogey, we immediately set a date to take it out in the yard on the first clear night. As luck would have it, tonight was perfectly clear, so when it got dark, Nathan, Matthew and I took the Mogey and the spyglass out to the back yard where Hiram joined us, as he often does for these stargazing outings. Nathan commented privately to me several times about how dark the sky was and how many stars are visible compared to the future, when the bright city lights and smoke-polluted skies make the hobby a less convenient one.

I've always been fascinated by a group of deep sky objects called the Messier Objects, a list of 109 galaxies, nebulae and clusters of stars that were catalogued in the late 1700's by a French astronomer. Messier was a comet hunter and to avoid confusing other things for comets, he started a list of these "other things" and their locations in the sky. He is remembered today more for this list than for any of the few comets he discovered. I started looking at the Messier Objects with the spyglass when I was in high school, but could only see the brighter ones. With the Mogey, I can see all but the faintest ones. It's just not big enough to pull in enough light for those.

There was no moon in the sky while we were out, so it was a good night to look for fainter objects, such as the Messiers, and that's what we did. By the time we finished, we had seen three galaxies (M81, M82 and M51, the spiral galaxy), three globular clusters (M3, M10 and M13) and the Ring Nebula (M57). A couple of these were pushing the limits of the Mogey's capability, but the dark clear sky made the difference. With the possible exception of a newborn baby I can't think of any of God's creations more awe-inspiring than a globular cluster. Every time I look through a telescope at a globular cluster, I have to remind myself to start breathing again.

Chapter 18

Diary entry

June 21, 1924

It's Saturday and another late start for me this morning after a late night of stargazing. Only a few months ago, when I was a much younger man, I could stay up with my telescope until the rising sun washed away the stars, then get a couple hours sleep and be off to work. Those days are memories now, and stamina eludes me.

Hiram was done at the bank at noon, so he, Nathan and I met at Mish's for lunch. Several of the regulars were there, as well as a few more shoppers than we normally see during the week. We hadn't yet discussed an agenda for the day, so I asked Nathan what he would like to do. He responded almost immediately that he would like to see the lakes I had told him about in my letters. It was a warm day, and I couldn't believe I hadn't come up with the idea myself. When we finished eating, Nathan walked to the hotel to change into more leisurely clothes, and Hiram and I headed up Main Street to do the same. I found an old bathing suit that should fit Nathan, and a few minutes later, with my son Matthew along, we picked him up and headed east on US 6.

The twenty-mile trip is a much easier one now than when I was a kid and we had to do it by horse and buggy over roads that were much more primitive than today. Then we would make a day of it, leaving home early in the morning and returning by evening, exhausted. Now it takes about forty minutes each way, and we make the trip every couple of weeks.

We headed first to the Oakwood Hotel on the west side of Lake Wawasee. The public beach there is well maintained with convenient parking and easy access. Molly and I have stayed at the hotel a few times with Matthew; it's a great family get-away. It was a little crowded today, as expected on a warm and sunny summer Saturday. We swam for a while, or more accurately stated in my case, walked around in the cool water. When everyone had had enough, we grabbed some candy at the hotel's snack bar, and then drove a couple miles to the east shore of adjoining Syracuse Lake, where we rented a rowboat and fishing poles, and bought some bait.

Syracuse Lake can best be described as a sleepy little lake. It's only a couple miles in diameter, much smaller than Wawasee, which for some reason is much more bustling. It's a great place to fish, though, and my ambition has always been to own a cottage on the east shore, the side opposite the town of Syracuse. It's the last inhabitable part of the lake to develop, in spite of the fact that it has the only natural sand beach on the lake and walk-up access to the water. Civilization has worked its way around the shoreline from town, eastward along the steeper north shore, and the south shore is mostly railroad right-of-way and wetlands.

Matthew was delighted to let Nathan help him bait his hook. He failed to tell Nathan that both Hiram and I now make him do it himself. A subtle grin between Matthew and me acknowledged the special circumstances of the day. I sat there remembering fishing here with my grandfather, who taught me to bait my hook nearly thirty years ago, while now Nathan was baiting the hook of his own 5-year old grandfather.

After a couple hours in the sun, the men were getting sun-burned, and I of course was exhausted, so we packed up and headed back to Nappanee, where we found dinner waiting at the Ruhls'. How lucky we are to live by such good friends.

After dinner, we said goodnight to our friends and walked across Main Street to our home. Nathan and I sat for a while in the back yard, talking and not talking. It was then that I first brought up the condition of his disfigured hand. He hesitated before responding, I sensed not out of embarrassment as much as because he didn't know what to say. Eventually he told me he had started this trip with a normal hand, and that the disfigurement happened during reassembly in the transporter, similar to Spot's experience. As a result, he now had some new apprehension about the return trip, and there was nothing he could do to modify the equipment, partially because all of his equipment was in 2003, and partly because of fear of really messing something up and stranding himself here in 1924.

Chapter 20

Diary entry

June 25, 1924

The transporter was scheduled to leave sometime in the afternoon, so Nathan's plan was to be waiting for departure inside it no later than 10:00AM. He was sitting in the kitchen having breakfast when I came downstairs at 8:00. He waited patiently while I ate my breakfast, but was not totally successful in concealing his apprehension. I did my best to eat faster than my normal slow pace, and soon we were in the garage along with the few items Nathan had decided to take back with him. I unlocked the closet door and opened it.

The closet was empty.

Chapter 21

I can't begin to describe the instantaneous feeling of helplessness that came over me as I realized that the transporter had apparently gone home without Nathan. Without Nathan in the future to send the transporter back to us, was there any hope of Nathan ever getting home to the year 2003? If Nathan had the same fears, he didn't verbalize them, and almost immediately said, "Let's get busy. We have work to do."

Nathan's plan was one he had worked out as a contingency should the automatic transporter retrieval not work. He explained it to me as he started unscrewing the panel in the back of the closet. The transporter controls had been programmed to automatically send the transporter back to 1924 again in 24 hours if he didn't intervene. The remote control apparatus behind the panel would then be reprogrammed to retrieve the transporter six hours later.

As I have come to expect of Nathan, he also had a back-up to his back-up plan. He would send a letter to his lab assistant via Garrison & Krebbs as I had done many times communicating with Nathan. Nathan's assistant had not been involved with any of the time travel experiments, and in fact didn't know of the project's existence. He was, however, already on alert that if he hadn't seen Nathan on schedule, he should look for the letter at Garrison & Krebbs' office and proceed according to the instructions in the letter. Nathan would instruct him how and when to send the transporter, then retrieve it again six hours later. I was starting to feel relieved.

Nathan pulled the back panel out of the way to reveal the electronic gizmo I described earlier. He touched one of several buttons on a small panel, and a series of small blinking lights somehow told Nathan that a No. 31 fault had occurred, whatever that was. He explained as he worked that something had caused a small voltage deviation in one of the timing circuits. He removed a small cover and a smile broke out on his face. "A little bug tells me you've seen this apparatus before, Josiah. Did your curiosity get the better of you?"

Busted. How did he know that I had snooped?

"Don't worry about it. I'm sure I would have looked behind the panel myself had I been in your shoes. Let me show you what happened," and he proceeded to describe what I was now looking at legitimately. He pointed to a fly that had been fried between two parallel plates. "This part of the device receives a signal when the transporter arrives, and the return instructions are programmed in at that moment. Since flies only live a few days at most, this little guy had to have sneaked into this sealed compartment in the few days before I arrived last week. He could only have gotten in if the panel was removed. It's his misfortune that he happened to be between the flux plates when the juice flowed. The good news is that the transporter did leave, just earlier than planned. In all likelihood, it arrived in 2003 early by the same amount of time. I'm very confident that the bus will be back again tomorrow. Now, let's put this closet back together and get that letter written."

Later this afternoon, Nathan met Joe Garrison.

Chapter 22

Diary entry

June 26, 1924

It was with great difficulty that I crawled out of bed this morning. I am very tired all the time now. I'm lucky that I was able to get the swim in Saturday; I fear it could be my last. I wore myself out that day and have recovered little since.

Nathan had come over at about 8:00, before I was up, and checked the garage closet. No transporter yet, but he didn't expect it until around 10:00 or so. He had a window of about six hours to get into the transporter once it arrived, and he planned to sit in it from the moment he found it in the closet until it left for the return. I finished breakfast a little before 10:00, and we checked the closet again. What a relief to see the transporter sitting there as if it had been there all along.

Nathan loaded his few belongings into
the cage and we said our good-byes, with the
promise that he would contact me by mail with
his plan for the next trip. He locked the door
from the inside with his key, and I walked
slowly toward town. Walking was more
difficult today, not just because I was tired, but
I had to make a conscious effort to lift my feet
high enough. Twice I stumbled as my feet
dragged along the sidewalk.

I was a day later than I had intended
to be in going back to the store, and although Ira
didn't complain, he was obviously relieved to
have some help bringing the books up to date. I
warned him as the day wore on that he was
going to be taking over completely probably
sooner than we had anticipated. I couldn't make
it past 2:00, and Ira called Hiram to pick me
up and drive me the two blocks home. It was the
first time ever that I hadn't walked it. Hiram
dropped me off and said he would come over in
the evening to play checkers if I felt like it.
When he drove into his garage, I ducked into
mine to see if Nathan was still around. I called
to him through the door, and when there was no
response, opened the door to find the closet
empty. I hope his trip was a safer one this time.
I went into the house through the back door to

avoid Hiram seeing me, kissed Molly hello, and passed out on the couch until she woke me for dinner three hours later.

I felt a little better after my nap and a good dinner, and true to his word, Hiram checked in on me later and we played checkers while Molly and Mary Ellen did whatever they do in the kitchen.

Chapter 23

Diary entry

June 27, 1924

    I think I almost didn't wake up this morning. I woke very gradually with a buzzing ringing sensation in my head, and the left side of my body still isn't working right. My speech is slightly slurred and my left leg wants to drag when I walk. Molly was scared to death. Doc Kendall came over right away and asked me if I wanted to go to the hospital but didn't really encourage it. It looks like the beginning of the end, and I have too many things to finish to spend any time in the hospital.

    Hiram stopped by in the afternoon, and I asked him to drive me to Joe Garrison's office. I gave Joe what will probably be my last letter to Nathan while Hiram waited in the car.

Letter to Nathan

June 27, 1924

My dear great grandson,

      I'm writing this quickly to you while I am still able. I want first to thank you for including me in the adventure we've gone through over the last three months. I have never in my life been so excited and had so much fun. To be able to participate in a scientific discovery of this magnitude is more than I ever could have hoped. Secondly, I need to tell you that if I don't send you any more letters, it's not for lack of interest on my part. Cancer is quickly taking over my body, and I fear I will lose the battle soon. Today has seen a dramatic turn for the worse. I have suffered a small stroke, and the doctor is not encouraging with the prognosis. You probably know the date of my death from the papers in the library or from the family Bible, but I wanted to alert you personally. I suspect it's not a coincidence that you came to visit me when you did, and I can think of no better distraction in my waning weeks than to have first communicated, then visited with you.

Thanks for having made it so easy to forget my health problems.

I wish you the best in your future progress. I wish I could be there when you receive your Nobel Prize, as I have no doubt you will.

Your proud great-grandfather,

Josiah

Chapter 24

Diary entry

June 28, 1924

    I woke up again this morning. That trivial statement, which would have seemed a waste of time to write a few weeks ago, today carries a special significance to me. I'm grateful that it's true, and I'm grateful that I still have the strength to write it.

    The mailman brought a delightful surprise today, not one but three envelopes which I recognized to be from Nathan. They were numbered one, two, and three, so I opened them in that order.

Letter 1, received June 28, 1924

December 9, 2003

Dear Josiah,

I arrived home this morning after awaiting transport in the garage closet for only about two hours. The trip was better than uneventful. The phenomenon that caused my hand to deform on the trip to 1924 reversed itself on the return, and my hand appears to be back to normal again. Perhaps the same thing would happen to Spot if he were to make the return trip, but knowing how attached Matthew has become to him, I would never ask you to send Spot back now. Confirmation of that bit of scientific discovery can wait until another time.

I'm sorry to hear about your failing health. I hope your discomfort is not too bad. While we know you are able to read OK, I'm going to send you a couple more letters to bring you up to date on my future progress. You should have received them in the same delivery with this one, numbered chronologically. I don't know yet when I will write them; I'll wait until I have something interesting to say. Until then, I remain

Your humble great grandson,

Nathan

Letter 2, received June 28, 1924

July 29, 2006

Dear Josiah,

I've been very busy the last three years, refining both the A.L.T. process and time travel. It is now pretty routine to travel back to any era I want and return to the present. I've made two significant refinements to the apparatus. First, I've built the transporter so that it is self-contained and doesn't require the separate control module that is behind the panel in the closet. This makes the process much easier for returning to the present whenever I am ready, rather than preprogramming according to a fixed schedule. No more missed buses that way. Second, I've developed a safety shield that makes it impossible to reassemble in the space occupied by another object. It sort of nudges the object aside to prevent coexistence in the same space. This eliminates the need for only transporting to a fixed location such as the closet, and obviously opens up the horizons for travel to just about anywhere.

I have almost concluded that travel to the future is impossible, the "Second Law" of time travel. The apparent reason is that the future doesn't exist yet. Travel backward in time is possible because the past has existed, and returning to where you started, "the present", is possible because the transporter has already experienced the time in between. However, it has not been possible for me to take the transporter any further into the future than the time when the transporter left the present. The up side of this is that when returning to the present, it's very easy to get back to the precise moment you left, because you can't overshoot it, even if you try.

I've documented my experiments religiously. When I have time (no pun intended), I hope to write my memoirs. You will have a prominent role in my story, and I'll send you a copy when I finish it. More than likely before that happens, though, I'll send you another update on my progress. Until then, I remain

Your humble great grandson,

Nathan

Letter 3, received June 28, 1924

September 3, 2015

Dear Josiah,

As you predicted, I have won the Nobel Prize for Physics. I wish I could have brought you to my "present" to witness the ceremony, but I can't get around that Second Law of time travel. The award was actually for A.L.T. and its applications in the instantaneous and inexpensive moving of people and things around the country and around the world. Its impact on transportation has been staggering.

I have kept my time travel studies private. You and I are the only people to know about the project, and I will probably keep it that way. I have too many fears that it will be misapplied and really screw up our lives, so unless somebody else develops it independently, as they certainly may, the secret will die with me. I have also decided not to write my memoirs. Time travel was what I was excited to write about, and without the time travel, my memoirs would be too dull for anyone to want to read. So, if you only get three letters today, that's the reason. The promised memoirs aren't going to happen.

If I do anything else interesting, I'll write you again with an update. I've given you enough to think about for one day, so I'll send the next to arrive in a few days.

Get your rest, and I look forward to hearing from my penpal soon.

All the best,

Nathan

Chapter 25

Diary entry

June 28, 1924 (cont.)

I knew I would never hear from him again. Nathan knows when I am going to die, and if it's not imminent, why would he send me three letters today? I'm not sad; I'm just very tired. I've had more than my share of good times in my life, many of them in the past few weeks. I have a loving wife and a caring and sensitive son to carry on for me, a best friend across the street whom I have had the pleasure to know all my life, and last, but not least, a great grandson coming along who will make the family name live in infamy. How could a pharmacist in a little country town in Indiana expect more?

Now I have to write a letter to Hiram.

Afterword

By Hiram Ruhl
July 26, 1934

Josiah died on July 3, 1924, less than a week after he wrote his last letter to me, the letter with which I started this story. He said little to anyone in the last few days. He was very weak, but seemed very much at ease with himself and his plight. There were few tears by anyone until it was over. The funeral accomplished the one purpose that I have come to appreciate those morbid events for; we were able to say goodbye to a dear friend with a finality that otherwise would not be realized.

We all tried to get on with our lives. I had the crutch of my job to lean on, to distract me during the days from thoughts of our loss. Molly had the tougher chore, that of bracing herself to repeat the same ordeal with her son. Soon after Josiah's cancer had been diagnosed, Molly had learned that Matthew also was afflicted and faced the same fate. His form of the disease was leukemia, dreaded killer of children. Whether or not there was a genetic link between his and his father's diseases is not known and may never be known, but the common denominator was the grief of the mother and wife Molly.

Molly had managed very successfully to conceal his son's condition from Josiah. Matthew showed only occasional and slight symptoms that were easily passed off as normal childhood illnesses. Molly had taken Mary Ellen and me into her confidence soon after Matthew's diagnosis was made. The grief was more than even she wanted to bear alone, and I assigned myself the task of doing everything I could to make their lives as normal as possible.

The plan came to me over the course of a few days and continued to evolve after I put it into action. As should be obvious to you by now, Josiah was never to have a great grandson, because his only child would not live to be a parent. Nathan Josiah Webb was a figment of my imagination, created to occupy my best friend's thoughts and distract him from his pain. The plan had the side benefit of helping to conceal his son's similar fate, implying that Matthew was to reach a normal adulthood, continuing the chain of descendants that eventually would include Josiah's great grandson. And it kept me busy. I have never worked so hard in my life. I'm not very creative, and trying to imagine new things to write to Josiah was much more of a chore than I expected it to be. I know the distraction was as good for me as it was for anyone. Not once during the four month long charade did I ever feel helpless to do anything about his dying, because I knew that I was doing everything I could.

I was sitting on the porch swing one evening after supper, drinking coffee and watching everything and nothing that was going on. Over the course of half an hour, a few neighbors meandered by on the sidewalk and waved. I could see the bank and the pharmacy down the street a couple blocks, and watched Sy Miggs drop a letter in the mailbox hanging on the store wall. That's when the idea popped into my head. It was probably triggered also by the postcard photograph of the downtown area I see for sale at all the downtown stores. The mailbox shows up prominently on that postcard. Whatever the stimulus, watching Sy mail that letter was the exact moment it popped into my head. Send Josiah a letter from the future. I didn't get the whole plan in a flash. If I had, I would have been spared a lot of mental machinations, but the basic idea was there. I got excited about it immediately, because the concept was as intriguing to me as it eventually became to Josiah.

I never could have pulled it off without the help of Joe Garrison. He was in on it from the start. How he managed to accept those letters from Josiah with a straight face is beyond me, but he did, and Josiah was never the wiser. Joe was the only other person (except, of course, "Nathan") who knew about my project.

Opening the letters, reading them, and resealing them in case Josiah ever wanted to revise them proved to be both time-consuming and painstaking. It's funny how little details like that turn into such obstacles to progress. I steamed that first envelope till I was afraid it would disintegrate, but diligence finally paid off. I eliminated that problem by doctoring Josiah's remaining envelopes by wetting the glue, then blotting much of it off before it redried. Subsequent openings and resealings proved to be much easier than the first. And did you ever wonder while reading the story how I had access to Josiah's letters and inserted them into the story line when the letters should have been with Nathan in the future? That was a chink in the armor of the story being believable, but of course, in reality, I had all of the letters after Joe Garrison emptied the file drawer after Josiah's death.

One idea of my plan turned out to solve a lot of problems for me. I had struggled with thoughts of how to pull off the arrivals and departures of the time traveling objects. The closet in the garage made it all easy to accomplish. The panel-covered space in the back of the closet allowed me to do several things. First, the screws allowed fairly easy removal and replacement of both the panel and the ceiling. I built the transporter out of steel tubing, with loose folding joints which allowed it to be compressed backward into a structure about a third of the depth of the original. This way, when the transporter was supposedly in the "future", it was actually behind the panel, doubling as the structure of the control module. The controls themselves were made from an assortment of electrical parts I got from Lamar Stoops at the phone company. They didn't do anything except for some lights blinking when Nathan did his "diagnostics."

Josiah made the charade easier when he gave Nathan a key to the closet. I had originally planned to remove the ceiling panel and climb down into the closet from above the garage rafters, but Josiah simplified that part of the plan. It was much easier to walk through the door.

The time that Josiah spent building the garage closet allowed me time to build the transporter and controls. I needed every hour to keep up with my end of the deception. The letter reading and writing had occupied all of my free time up to that point. I was happy to redirect the effort to the actual transport phase of the project, because I was running out of things to write.

Once the garage closet was built, I had the added complication of moving things in and out of the garage without being noticed, especially by Josiah or Molly. I timed most of the deliveries to coincide with Josiah's work schedule, so he wasn't too difficult. Sometimes I was able to see Molly leaving the house, but usually I was just lucky that Molly never noticed. When I could, I would move things in and out at night, but I was afraid that luxury would stop after Spot arrived. Fortunately, he recognized me even in the dark and didn't bark at me.

Getting Spot into the closet was a little more difficult than the smaller objects. He was pretty excited about being carried in the cage, and left a little present on the garage floor before I got the closet door open. Fortunately, I had enough time to clean up the mess before Josiah came home for lunch that day.

Nathan's visit was part of my plan almost from the beginning, certainly before I had worked out how I was going to get him here from "the future". Nathan is actually a casual friend of mine, Stanley Miller, whom I met at a banking convention several years ago. He is semi-retired, reportedly having made a small fortune early in his career. He lives in Ft. Wayne, Indiana and was born with a slightly deformed left hand. I thought the hand would add to the intrigue of the perils of time travel. Stan hadn't met Josiah and didn't know anyone else in Nappanee and was an eager participant. We only had one close call with Stan seeing one of his neighbors when we went to Lake Wawasee. He was able to avoid being noticed and we got through the rest of the day without incident.

The fact that Stan is a Cubs fan was a plus and made several of the conversations easier. Josiah's impression that Nathan had done his homework in preparing for his trip to the past amused me. If only Josiah had known that discussing the future was the hard part for Nathan. We had decided in anticipating questions about the future that Nathan would generalize as much as possible, and if backed into a corner would fall back on not wanting to be too specific for fear of somehow influencing change. It turned out not to be a serious problem, and Stan was able to wing it quite well.

Another potential problem also didn't materialize. Stan's writing is so different from mine that I was afraid Josiah might notice. I typed all the letters from Nathan, only signing his name by hand, and Stan was able to mimic the signature well enough, so we averted the problem.

Stan didn't know the first thing about astronomy, so the night of our barbecue at Josiah's, after Josiah went to bed and I walked Nathan back to town, I taught him the rudiments about telescopes and the June night sky. The timing was good; the very next night we had our observing night, and he was able to keep up with the conversation. Those observing nights are some of my best memories of Josiah, and I miss them sorely. Molly knows how much both Josiah and I enjoyed those times together, and the day she gave me the box with the diary and letters, she also asked me to come over to the house and get the Mogey telescope. It's in the corner of my office at home now, and I see it every time I sit down at my desk. It's a very pleasant reminder of my old friend, and I find myself gazing at it often.

The delay by one day of Nathan's return to the future was injected into the plan to add a little suspense, and I think it did just that. It required a little planning ahead of time, stuffing a dead fly between the capacitor plates, but that was easy. Stan still chuckles when he talks about the looks on Josiah's face, first when he realized that the transporter wasn't there and later when he thought he had been busted after snooping behind the panel. I had banked on Josiah's curiosity getting the better of him, as it did, but even if he hadn't peeked we would have used the fried fly as the reason for the equipment malfunction.

We were very fortunate in timing Nathan's visit. One week later and it would have been too late. Josiah had a series of strokes after the first one and was totally incapacitated within a couple days after Nathan's departure. It was almost as if Nathan knew from the library records when Josiah would die, but as you now know, of course, we were just lucky.

To this day, I have not told this story to anyone, not even Molly. Joe Garrison knows only as much as he needed to know to play his part, and he is sensitive enough about my relationship with Josiah never to have brought it up again after I picked up the contents of the file drawer from his office. Both Joe and Stan agreed not to share the tale with anyone else, and I'm confident they've kept their word. The story is recorded now, but I doubt that it will ever go beyond this box. It's a very personal thing between my best friend Josiah and me. I'll probably read it from time to time to refresh my memories of him and this last adventure together, though I doubt I'll ever need a reminder. I miss you, old friend, and look forward to catching up with you at some as yet unknown time in "the future".

Hiram

Author's Notes

By John Ruhl
February 20, 2004

The embellishments to which I referred in the Preface are limited to changes I made in describing modern day events. When he was writing the letters from Nathan, my great grandfather Hiram could not have known about the space race of the '60's or that the Cubs wouldn't win a World Series in the time span covered by this story. I replaced his inaccurate speculations about life in the year 2003 (300 mph hover cars, for instance) with events that really did occur. My motivation in making these changes was to allow the reader to be drawn into the story as Josiah was. To include inaccurate "historical" facts would have served to alert the reader prematurely to the fictional nature of the time travel aspect of Hiram's ruse.

Josiah's house is gone now, razed and replaced some thirty years ago by a medical building, but Hiram's is still standing across Main Street. It's now a Bed & Breakfast, as are many of the fine old homes in town. Nappanee itself was a great place to grow up, and it retains the charm for which it has been known for over a century. It's not difficult, while walking down any of a dozen or more streets, to imagine the town as it was in Josiah and Hiram's 1924.

The story itself is an intertwining of fact and fantasy. You the reader are encouraged to draw the line between the two wherever that line creates the best story for you.

The Mogey telescope in my dining room now has new significance to me, and like my great grandfather Hiram, I find myself gazing at it often as I recall snippets of the history it has witnessed. I hope all of you can find similar links of your own to remind you of your families' stories.

The End

To order additional copies of this book, you may do so at our website, www.MajorMicroPress.com, where you will find current pricing, shipping and sales tax rates, if applicable. The website also has mail order instructions for those who prefer this method. Quantity discounts are available.